Not Today Not Any Day

Not Today
Not Any Day

Nikki

www.hispenpublishing.com

Douglasville, Georgia

This is a work of fiction. The characters, incidents, and dialogues are products of the author's imagination and are not to be construed as real. Any references to actual events, persons, living or dead, or to real locales are intended to give the novel a sense of reality.

Not Today, Not Any DAy
Published by His Pen Publishing, LLC
Douglasville, Georgia 30134

Copyright ©2017 by Nikki

ISBN: 978-1-944643-13-3

Library of Congress Control Number: 2018945036

First Printing

Printed in the United States of America

This book is also available in digital eBook format

Dedication

To my mother Jacquelyn,
Sheldon, Robert, and a
host of family members
and friends.

Acknowledgments

First, I would like to thank GOD for blessing me. Second, I would like to thank my friends who shared their stories with me and allowed me to fictionally dramatize their relationships in writing. Finally, I would like to thank my family for their support and encouragement. A special thanks to Shana Burton who took time from her busy schedule to encourage me and advise me from an author's perspective.

Table of Contents

Introduction

Today or Any Day: He's Not the One

Damn! Not another one! Yep you heard right. Another relationship gone to hell because he wouldn't act right. I am so tired of these stupid ass guys in relationships. The purpose of this book is to allow me to vent about why and how the men in my life lost me. The men thought they had done all of the right things that a man is supposed to do but I left anyway. What happened and why?

Well, let's just keep it real because I am about to let it all hang out. It wasn't about the sex like most of them might think. It was because of what they *weren't* doing in the other rooms of the house, not the bedroom. Little do they know that "laying the pipe" in the bedroom is not a guarantee that a woman is going to stay. She may enjoy the pipe but he could still end up being the temporary playmate until she accepts another application. By the time he realizes that he has been stupid, it's usually already too late—she's gone and there is nothing to be done but accept that fact.

In a woman's eyes, being good to her is totally different from being good to her in a man's eyes. Most of the men I encountered believed being a good man meant working, chipping in with the bills, dating occasionally, and giving her some of the things she wanted. They had a provider/protector mentality. They thought if they did a few good things, then it would negate all of the wrongs they did and I would be grateful to have "a man like him." He thought he could treat me any kind of way and because I loved him, I would stay with him no matter what. Oh, and heaven forbid because I'm a plus size woman, I should be happy to get a man! He tried to convince me I couldn't get anyone else.

Note to men: Use your brain. If you wanted her, someone else will too. You are not the only man in the world even if she makes you feel that way.

I believe one of the biggest lies that's ever been told in the relationship world is, "You never know what you have until it's gone." That statement is some real bull. Most people in relationships know exactly what they have, but they never thought the person would leave. I've heard men say too many times things like, "She's not going anywhere or she's just mad right now, she'll be alright, she's just going through something. It'll pass." All along, she's been telling him things that should have gotten his attention. However, like most men, he was so busy doing his thing that he never stopped to realize he had forced her to do hers.

Most relationships in turmoil go through five stages of grief: denial, anger, bargaining, depression, and acceptance. These stages of grief are not guaranteed to be in this order but they are all present. However, once the person has gone through them, the relationship is usually completely done.

Denial: Recognize their behavior change even though you don't want to believe you're being cheated on or being mistreated. It may be hard to admit because you can't believe they would do you that way. No matter how you slice it, this is a form of abuse. When I say abuse, I don't always mean physical abuse. There are other forms of abuse, which can be emotional and mental. Some of us have even ignored it by pretending the other woman or the abuse doesn't exist until we are forced to face it. This is how we are forced to face these issues:

A. Someone sees him with the other woman and informs you.

B. His playmate informs you of his play activities because she wants him for herself.

C. You catch him outright.

D. His playmate gives him and you something you didn't ask for (i.e., STD or baby)

Anger: This is self-explanatory, but you lash out at him.

You argue constantly. You are outraged because nothing is right in the relationship. There is a continuous explosion of rage and disappointment. You become argumentative about even the smallest things. Most of the time, he calls it being emotional or he thinks it's because you're on your cycle.

Bargaining: This is when you give him an ultimatum. It may be that he needs to choose, end an affair, or meet some type of deadline. You may even give him a timeframe to comply. You allow him time to explain to his playmate things are going to end. You may give him time to change or show some form of improvement in his actions towards you.

Depression: This is when you may become silent. You cry privately or sometimes to your friends. You become introverted and don't want him to touch you. You become non-responsive in the bedroom, that is, if you are still sleeping with him. You start eating a lot more or not at all. No matter how the depression shows itself, he needs to pay attention.

Acceptance: This is the real danger zone. If you have accepted his carousing, mistreatment, and neglect without complaint, then he is in serious trouble. Your relationship could be facing its demise.

He should have been paying attention instead of saying things like "she's tripping" or "it must be that time of the month again." Here are some signs most men take for granted and ignore.

Hint #1 - She complains about being unhappy in the relationship.

Hint #2 - She complains she feels alone in the relationship.

Hint #3 – She is melancholy. She may sigh in despair and shake her head a lot.

Hint #4 - She stops complaining.

Hint #5 - She stops caring about what he does, where he goes, and when he's coming back. She may even encourage him to go.

Hint #6 – She becomes silent until, finally, she leaves.

Now ladies *and* men, I don't want you to perceive this as a man-hating book because this is not. This is just my way of discussing the most frustrating crap that occurs in relationships and situationships. Some men might take offense to what they read while others may feel if they had known then what they just found out, they may not have gone through the drama that occurred in the relationship.

As I contemplated writing this book, I surveyed several of my male friends. They told me they wished they had this insight into women earlier because they learned about some of the mistakes they made and decided to make immediate changes. They started paying attention.

Chapter 1

The Wanna Be Player

To the "wanna be player" who thought he had me right where he wanted me, know that you didn't. In reality, he found out he was the real fool. Being a smart woman, I will allow a man enough rope to hang himself, and just when he thinks I'm in his hands, he'll look up and I'll be gone. Not just gone from him but also gone with someone else. While he was busy in the streets with his other woman, and thought I was sitting at home complaining or unaware of his activities, keep in mind that someone else was listening to me. **Note: Sometimes you may have to play the fool to fool the fool who's trying to play you for a fool.**

There is always a friend or someone who sees the best in a woman and knows how big a fool the man was for treating you the way he did. They are patiently waiting for her to notice them. By the time your mate realizes what has happened, he may accuse you of cheating when that is not the truth. He was so busy doing his thing and thought you would never leave him. Actually, he was the one who opened the door and pushed you out.

When I finally left, it was right into the arms of someone else. Of course, the man's thought process says, *"She left without warning. She was cheating all along. She was no good."* In reality, there were warnings, but he obviously chose not to see them. Instead, he chose to keep doing the same old things. He chose the heartbreak he now faced.

While he was out in the streets chasing other women, he never thought that someone would be chasing his woman and that she could be caught. He forgot she was smart, calm, cool, calculating, and conniving.

At first, you may be emotional and irrational, but then you stop allowing your emotions to control the situation and begin to think, ponder, and calculate. I strategized the best method to change my circumstances. I left him subtle clues to awaken his senses to the coming demise, hoping he would see the error of his ways. I gave him a chance to straighten up. However, most men fail to recognize this can happen to them. They think "she would never do that to me." By the time reality sets in, he has been bamboozled, but he did it to himself. Remember Johnnie Taylor's song because it's so true...*Who's making love to your old lady while you're out making love.*

Here's my story:

WARNING: She's smarter than you think so don't assume she won't leave.

The Player Got his Heart Broken

Shawn was cute and fine, the ideal sexy man women like. He was tall, with washboard abs of a Greek god, and a pecan tan. He had a Barry White voice and was bowlegged. The man was so fine that he could have been on TV with those abs. When you looked at him, you had to do a double take and pick your chin up off the floor.

He had a woman he truly cared about. Her name was Tonya. However, he had Sheila too. Tonya was the woman he helped to pay bills, took care of her and her kids, took on dates publicly, and took home to his mama. Sheila was one of his playmates. I say *one of his playmates* because there were others. He sometimes took Sheila around his family, too. He took Sheila to places he and Tonya didn't go because Sheila had more expensive taste.

Shawn was so smooth that when Tonya found out about Sheila, she initially tried to fight Sheila over him. Sheila knew he was no good but he was fun to play with. Poor Tonya was in love. The *story goes like this:*

Sheila, a middle school teacher, was standing outside a building with her students as they participated in a fundraiser when Shawn walked up. They admired each other and spoke as he passed. She continued to work with the children and he walked into the building. When Shawn came out the building he stopped to talk to one of her students. Sheila, being protective of the children, wanted to see why he had engaged her student. As it turned out, Shawn was the student's older brother. The student introduced them to each other.

Being the charismatic type of guy Shawn was, he flashed his beautiful, pearly white teeth and greeted Sheila with a polite kiss on her hand. Shawn was in a relationship with Tonya when he met Sheila, but he still wanted her. They became engaged in conversation and enjoyed talking to each other. At the end of the conversation, Shawn asked for Sheila's phone number and they began a relationship.

As months progressed, Shawn started spending more time with Sheila, practically living at her house. He told her he was looking for a mate. He stopped going to Tonya's house and began going to Sheila's house and spending the night. Sheila had no clue Tonya existed, nor did she know Shawn was going to Tonya's house before he went to work.

Tonya noticed a change in Shawn. "So what's going on, Shawn?" Tonya asked.

"What do you mean?"

"Don't play stupid. Where have you been? What have you been up to?" Tonya knew him like a book. Something was different with his behavior.

"I haven't been up to nothing. I've been going to my dad's house after work."

Tonya believed there must be another woman. She began to scheme and plan to find the other woman. One evening, she went to Shawn's father and told him she had left something in Shawn's room. His dad was used to seeing Tonya and having her spend the night sometimes with his son. He allowed Tonya into Shawn's room. She rambled through Shawn's belongings until she found Sheila's phone number.

At about two o'clock in the morning, Tonya called Sheila. This was not going to be good.

Sheila jumped up, almost in a panic, because of the hour of night. She answered the phone. "Hello!"

"Hey, my name is Tonya. I'm looking for my boyfriend, Shawn. Is he there?"

"Excuse me?"

"I heard he was with you tonight. Is that true?"

"Ummm, hold on a moment. Shawn, wake up."

"Huh?"

"Shawn, wake up. Telephone!"

Shawn answered the phone and pretended to be so groggy that he couldn't complete the conversation and passed the phone back to Sheila. Tonya began yelling like a banshee because this was not the first time she found out Shawn was cheating.

"Hello, this is Sheila. You said that you were his girlfriend? How did you get my number?"

"Actually, I'm his fiancé. He's been dating the both of us."

"I understand you're upset with him but I don't appreciate you calling my house at this hour with drama. Thank you for informing me, but do not call my house again." Sheila, pissed, slammed the phone down. She was shocked. She attempted to wake Shawn up again. Shawn pretended to be asleep.

Sheila was furious. She tried a third time to wake him up, but again he didn't move. She kicked Shawn so hard he flipped out of bed, hit the wall, and slid to the floor. He looked like someone had taken a fly swatter and smacked him against a window.

He jumped up and asked, "What's going on?"

"Are you awake now?" Although Sheila was mad as hell, inside, she laughed at the way he hit the wall. She thought, *I should have videoed that*. "We need to talk right now. Who is Tonya?"

"My ex-girlfriend. She's been stalking me. She's plain crazy. I don't want her."

Sheila, although feeling like he was lying, temporarily accepted his explanation. She continued to see Shawn but she became curious about Tonya. Sheila wondered if what Tonya said about her and Shawn was true.

Sheila was smart. All she had to do was ask and she would receive. She went back to her roots...church. She began to pray and look for the truth. She knew without a doubt that God would reveal everything she needed to know.

Shawn, oblivious to Shelia's suspicions, continued the charade he was playing. He had no clue that on this particular day Sheila watched as he got into Tonya's car ten minutes after getting out of her car. He rode to Tonya's house and stayed for a few hours, and then Tonya drove him to work. Sheila watched as he and Tonya passionately kissed goodbye. He got out of Tonya's car and disappeared inside the building.

Sheila sat in her car stunned, hurt, and disappointed. Tonya had told the truth after all. Tears rolled down her face. She went home in utter dismay, distraught and heartbroken. The man she thought she had built a relationship with was nothing but a liar, but Sheila was a praying woman. She didn't discuss her relationship with Christ with many people, but whenever things started to get rough, she turned more and more to God. He was her source and solace. As she poured out her heart to God, she asked for guidance and direction. She knew without a doubt He would take her where she needed to go. Sheila decided she and Tonya needed to meet face to face for a woman-to-woman discussion.

She contacted Tonya. The ladies decided to make their meeting interesting. They met at the same restaurant where Shawn worked. They both agreed not to tell him of his impending doom. When they arrived at the restaurant and came face to face, the ladies shook hands and walked into the restaurant together.

The ladies sat together and conversed about their connection to Shawn. He was in the kitchen so he didn't see them. The ladies decided to go and wait outside of the restaurant for Shawn to get off work.

As he walked out of the restaurant after his shift ended, He looked around and noticed both Sheila and Tonya outside of the restaurant. He proceeded to go and get into Sheila's car. She told him to go to Tonya. He walked over to Tonya and cursed her out. He embarrassed her beyond measure and called her everything but a child of God.

Sheila was mortified to see this display. He made it abundantly clear to Tonya that he was with Sheila, much to Sheila's surprise. He told Tonya to go home and to stop stalking him because it was over. Tonya left the restaurant in defeat.

For the next few weeks, Shawn pampered Sheila with flowers, massages, dinners, and shopping. He wanted to show her she was the only woman for him. That was short lived. He was simply trying to lull Sheila back into a place of comfort so he could go back to his old routine.

Shawn didn't realize the trust between him and Sheila was broken. Sheila was no longer following Shawn; she had gotten her strength to follow God.

Shawn wasn't worried about Tonya. He could get her back anytime. Once he thought Sheila showed signs of trusting him again, he went back to Tonya and drew her back in, too. Before long, he was up to his usual tricks.

As time progressed, Tonya began to harass Sheila by calling her house and leaving messages on her answering machine, calling at all hours of the night, early morning, and showing up at Shawn's job when she knew he was with Sheila. This time Sheila was the wiser.

For months, Sheila appeared to walk around confused, saddened, and heartbroken. After the realization that Shawn was never going to change, she decided to let him trap himself.

She refused to be the fool any longer. She was going to get even with her own personal revenge. Meanwhile,

Sheila met a guy named Tim. She was unaware that Tim and Shawn worked together and knew each other. Several weeks passed and Tim told her he worked with Shawn. Tim listened to her and became her friend. They talked a lot but never about Shawn. He never informed Sheila about Shawn's activities. Over time, Tim and Sheila began to hang out when Shawn was at work or up to his usual tricks. At first, Sheila wasn't sure if Tim was her friend or a distraction.

Tim admired Sheila and secretly wished they could be a couple instead of Sheila and Shawn but he did nothing to act on the feelings he had for her. He simply became a very good friend to Sheila.

Meanwhile, Shawn, in his mindless comfort zone, was unaware Sheila and Tim spent time together. He caroused around thinking that Tonya and Shelia were his. He was being his usual self when he and Tonya had a major blowout of an argument and he stormed out of her house. He called Uber and headed straight for Sheila's house. =

Sheila began to see that Shawn was not for her. Tim was the one who treated her like she wanted and needed to be treated. By this time, Sheila had accepted the fact that this was a lifestyle Shawn and Tonya were used to but she refused to be a part of it any longer. She wanted nothing else to do with Shawn. She made up in her mind she was going to end things with him and see how things worked out between her and Tim.

When Shawn arrived at Sheila's house, he saw Tim's car in the driveway. *That can't be Tim's car.* He knocked on Sheila's door several times but she didn't answer. He called her from his cell but she didn't answer.

Sheila and Tim were inside her house. They heard Shawn's knock and Sheila hit Ignore when he called. Sheila and Tim were discussing the best method of telling Shawn about their relationship. They decided they would invite him into the house.

Sheila opened the door and invited Shawn to come inside. Shawn walked into the house and paused. He was both stunned and pissed at the same time. "Why is Tim over here. How do you two know each other?"

Sheila immediately re-directed the conversation and asked Shawn, "Where have you been?"

Shawn avoided answering the question and turned to Tim. "Why are you over here, man? What the fuck's going on?"

Tim responded by going to Sheila and standing beside her. "Why didn't you answer her question?" he asked.

Shawn went into a tirade and accused Sheila of cheating on him with his friend. He accused them of messing around the entire time and suggested that Sheila was a loose woman with no moral standards. It never seemed to occur to him that he brought all of it on himself. He stormed out of the house.

As a last effort to save face, Shawn tried to make up with Tonya, but again the joke was on him because Tonya had been taking her own applications. She called Sheila and told her to keep Shawn but Sheila had her own news for Tonya. Shawn had been replaced in both places. He had to go home to his father's house—alone.

The moral of this story is you can be a playa and find yourself played. You can't chase women and keep the one you have indefinitely. It will catch up to you eventually.

Chapter 2

Hanging With the Boys

This next story deals with another type of idiot. Ladies, you know the one who neglects home for his friends because he doesn't want her to change him. He is the one who makes too much time for his boys. He is going to watch the games, go out for drinks, shoot pool, or ride motorcycles, etc. He reserves three or four days per week for his activities with them. He leaves his woman at home alone or with the kids. Now don't get it wrong, he is entitled to have some time out with the guys, but this cannot be so constant that his woman is being ignored.

Ladies, just in case you aren't sure if your man falls in this category, here's how you know:

1. Every Saturday, Sunday, Monday, and Thursday he is going to 'his boys' house to watch football.

2. Every Saturday he watches college football somewhere other than home or he is at home and he still ignores you. Sometimes he invites his friends over to the

house. He expects you to be the hostess without talking to you about it. He simply makes the announcement that they are on the way.

3. On Friday night, after work, he goes to happy hour until some strange hour in the night.

You may not mind the occasional night out with his friends. However, if at some point you start to mention things like "you've done that for the last few weeks," or "you did that the last time," these statements are a clear indication you not getting the attention you need from him. You are beginning to feel alone or left out. He has the nerve to say, "I am who I am and I'm not changing or jumping through hoops for nobody." This attitude needs to stop quickly or else it is going to cause a problem in the long run. Eventually, it can lead to arguments. After the arguments, you can eventually become tolerant of the fact that he is going out. Finally, you stop saying much at all, only a cordial conversation to keep peace. You already know you're tired of being tired of his bull.

Note: He is in the danger zone already and doesn't even know it.

I'll Pay Attention Later…. The Fellas are Calling

Since he was divorced and his kids were grown, he had

become accustomed to hanging out with the fellas. He had gotten into a routine of weekly activities that he and his boys participated in. They were football fans and watched every game together. Then it happened. He met Tina who loved the game as much as he did. He devoted all of his free time to her. This occurred all summer long. Tina grew accustomed to spending a lot of time with him.

One day, Tony told Tina about his weekly traditions and football schedule since the season was about to begin. At first, Tina thought this routine was for Sundays only, but soon she learned that wasn't quite right. Apparently, Tony had given time and attention to her because it wasn't football season. Tony didn't have a lot of money because he was injured on the job and was out of work on disability. He had a lawsuit pending concerning the injury. Consequently, he was on a limited income until his settlement was reached. He couldn't be the big spender because he just didn't have the money.

Tina still enjoyed spending time with him. It didn't matter that he didn't have a lot of money, he made her feel like a queen. They talked and played cards for hours. They enjoyed various television shows and movies. He often cooked and they ate their meals together and even prayed together. They travelled and fished together. It was fun being with him. Who knew that it would be short lived.

Tony finally received a large settlement from his lawsuit and got a new job, weeks before football season. He was finally able to see daylight financially. Everything changed.

Tony began living the nightlife and spending more time hanging with the fellas and less time with Tina. He began to treat the queen like a peasant. She was queen no more. Every Sunday, Monday, Thursday and some Fridays he went out with the fellas. He never invited her to come along.

At first, she was fine with him spending time with his friends since he couldn't before due to his financial situation, but it was becoming too much. He started lying about where he was going and where he had been. His whole behavior changed. He stood her up for several dates and never explained why he didn't show or call. He started to take his phone calls in the other room, whispering if he thought she was listening to his conversation, turning his phone over so she could not see any text messages he received. He seemed to have lost interest in her.

Tina was observant enough to know something wasn't right but she waited for enough evidence to be certain in her mind. Tina did the only thing she knew to do, she started praying. She asked God to show her the truth. She prayed for discernment. She had no doubt God would open her eyes to the truth.

Along with the changes in behavior was his sudden

change in attitude towards her. He started to treat her like she was a hindrance. He made degrading and downright rude comments. He told her he didn't need her, and he could do most things better than her. Basically, he claimed her life was better because he was there. Never did it occur to him that she was content with her life before he came into it. At this point, Tina began feeling as though Tony was attacking her verbally, like he was making deliberate attempts to tear her down. The question in her mind was *why*. She became sad and depressed. Her whole behavior and attitude changed. Even her appearance started going down slowly.

Repeatedly, time and time again, Tony felt the need to degrade Tina or create reasons for them to argue. She began to think she couldn't do anything right in his eyes. It seemed the more she tried the worse he tried to make her feel. She was going down fast. But God!

God places people in our lives right when we need them most. Tina ran into her friend, Cynthia. Cynthia invited her to church. Tina reluctantly went to church with Cynthia. Cynthia never asked Tina any questions. She simply waited for Tina to come to her. She prayed for Tina and her situation.

God heard her prayers because Tina began to get herself back together. As she regained her strength, she realized her problem was Tony. She stopped calling, texting, returning calls, or making any effort in his direction. She started going out more, hanging with her friends, and not being available to him. She decided that Tony was not the only one who could go out and enjoy life. The only reason she settled down in the first place was because Tony didn't have the money to go out. She was respecting his financial situation by not trying to put him in an awkward position. Since he no longer had time for her, she no longer made time for him. That's when the tables turned.

Tony began calling Tina just to make sure she was at home waiting on him. He called for days at a time but no Tina. He would text her repeatedly, but still there was nothing. Tina refused to allow Tony to determine her day. She was tired of him lying to her, standing her up for dates, criticizing her, and trying to make her feel bad.

Of course, Tony, blind to his own actions and unaware of how he contributed to this situation, wanted to know what was going on and demanded she explain her behavior. She told him openly and honestly how she felt and why. She told him about his negative comments, about him going out three and four nights a week, about them not going anywhere anymore, and about being lonely in their relationship.

His response floored her. "You can shove that right up your ass. I am who I am. I'm not changing or jumping through hoops for anyone. Either you accept me for who I am or not." At that moment, Tina knew the relationship was over.

Tony thought everything was going to be fine. In his eyes, they simply had a minor disagreement, but he was so far from reality. He stayed away from Tina for a few days until he thought she had cooled off. Little did he know, she wasn't cool, she was cold. She was ice cold. She was completely done. It never occurred to Tony that he had done irreparable damage to the relationship.

Tina began getting involved with other activities and making friends. There was one friend in particular that stood out to her. His name was Rick. While Tony was gallivanting all over town with the fellas, he was leaving Tina available. He thought she was sitting at home doing nothing. Boy, was he wrong!

While Tony was out, Tina invited Rick over to watch football. Rick took her out, too. Since Tony didn't have any more time for her, she didn't feel any obligation to him. Rick was giving her all of the attention that Tony didn't.

Rick thought Tina was the best thing since sliced bread. He was just what she needed when she needed it. They began to develop a special bond as friends.

Tina told Rick about Tony and his treatment towards her. She cried many tears on his shoulder. She loved Tony and couldn't understand why he had changed so drastically. Suddenly, she became aware of the truth: Tony needed her. He was using her and keeping her just in case he needed something just like he did when he didn't have his money or a job. Now that he was getting back on his feet, he no longer needed her. He even posted on his social media, "You have to let go of the one you love so they can find their way back to you." Tina actually saw this and laughed.

She no longer complained to Tony about feeling neglected by him. He failed to see that she was gone both mentally and emotionally. She stopped calling, texting, returning calls, or making any effort to stay in their relationship. Tony thought she would stay no matter what. The brother was clueless. Not only was she done with him, but she had moved on to someone else right under his nose and he didn't even know it.

For months, Tony continued calling Tina to make sure that everything was fine. She actually held their usual conversation as though nothing had changed. When Tony finally saw Tina's engagement announcement in the newspaper, reality smacked him in the face. She was gone!

WARNING: If they won't pay attention to you someone else will.

Chapter 3

Mr. Smooth Talker/Operator

I love running into this type of guy. He is the charismatic, smooth talking "slickster" who thinks he can talk his way out of anything. He has no idea that a real woman can smell his bullshit a mile away. I may appear to be absorbed into his silk but trust me, not for very long.

He seems to think because he behaves like the ideal gentleman he can get over. He never thought about the fact that I am smart and cunning. Pulling out chairs, opening car doors, and showering me with material things only gets him so far. Those things get monotonous over time, especially filled with empty rhetoric. He didn't realize until it was too late that if he wasn't going to spend the quality time needed to get to know and love me properly, then I would leave him too.

Calling me on the phone to tell me all those sweet things

he thinks I want to hear can only get him so far. Actions speak 10 times louder than words. He was blind to the fact that he can't make empty promises and expect me to sit around and wait on him when it is clear that he is smooth talking. A man who can't keep his word is not worth a hill of beans. You know I'm right.

I will tolerate a lot but a liar will fall short every time. I will allow him to lie to himself for as long as he wants and never pay what he is saying any attention. I may laugh in his face when he is offering some of his empty words. I may tell him he's full of shit if he catches me in the right mood on the right day. I might become sarcastic in my response to what he's saying. However, most smooth talkers think I am gullible and that they can say anything. That used car salesman act only works in the movies. Trust me.

While he is lying, trying to make me believe the lies he has convinced himself are true, I'm accepting applications from real men. Now don't get it wrong, I will go out with him, have dinner, etc., but believe me when I tell you he is not a serious contender. While he is playing games, you'd better believe I am coaching the game.

The funny thing about cunning women and arrogant men is that women allow these men the opportunity to make a complete fool of themselves. Some of us will help them do it and laugh about it. This is not an attempt to slam women. It's an effort to help men stop playing themselves.

We Are Just Friends

Jim was Mr. Honest. He was so cool. Everybody loved to chill with him because he was the type of guy who was laid back and not into a lot of women chasing. He just wanted friends, and he was friends with some of the most attractive females around. He made sure he laid the truth out there so no one would feel mistreated. He always made it clear he had a woman but if they wanted to hangout, it was okay. However, Jim was nothing more than a used car salesman pretending to be honest.

Jim and Ashley had been dating for several years but they had problems. The first problem that Ashley knew was that Jim was not always honest with her. She caught him many times in lies but never once told him that she knew.

The second problem was Ashley wanted to know where their relationship was going but Jim repeatedly gave her empty promises of engagement and possibly marriage.

Finally, Jim had no job security. Things were not concrete financially, so technically he wasn't ready for anything serious anyway.

During their separations, Jim went out, met, and dated other women, while Ashley pondered how to make things right between them. He always told the other women about Ashley and asked them not to speak to him if they saw him with her. He led these women into believing that the relationship issues were all her fault.

This was his time to sleep around, date, and manipulate as many women as he could before he and Ashley reconciled. They always reconciled and he assumed that they would again as usual. He would tell Ashley that he was going out but he never said with whom. He never went out to places where he knew Ashley went. He insisted that the women knew that they were only his friends.

Ashley became wise to his maneuvering and often wondered if it was on purpose. She began to take applications of her own. Jim wasn't looking for applicants because his heart was set on Ashley. He just wanted seasonal help, occasionally. Ashley began to ask him about their relationship more and more. She wanted him to step up and do the things he told her so many times before, especially when he was smooth talking to get back into her good graces.

Jim was noncommittal. He continued to offer Ashley the promise of a future but never any substance. Over time, Ashley grew tired of waiting. She started seeing a new guy. Jim began to think about settling down with Ashley. He asked her what she needed in order for them to go to the next level. She told him to get a real job, a place to live, and to show her some sign they were moving to the next level. Jim did just that. He got a job with job security and good benefits. He bought a house and put Ashley's engagement ring on lay-away. He was making plans for their future. By now he'd gotten excited because she was the woman for him. It was time for Jim to propose.

Jim planned a small, secluded, romantic getaway weekend where he was going to pop the question. Little did he know, it was too late. Ashley called him the day before the trip and asked him to come over to her house. When he arrived, they sat and began to converse.

Ashley told him she knew about the women he had been seeing, about how he had been lying to her. She told him their relationship was over. Jim was devastated. After all of this time, while he thought he was smooth talking her, she had caught up to him. She was no longer interested in hearing what he had to say. He begged her but to no avail. Ashley was done with him forever.

WARNING: He can smooth talk his way right out of the one he truly loves.

Chapter 4

Mr. Selfish

This is that piece of aggravation who only hears, sees, and follows his own point of view. No one else has a valued opinion or side. He typically rejects any idea of him ever doing anything wrong. If someone points it out to him, he will defend that wrong tooth and nail. He can find fault with everyone but himself. He thinks he is perfect. I don't know who lied to this fool. He tries to flip the conversation when someone is telling him about his faults. He justifies his wrongs by saying it is in response to another's actions. Child, he is so perfect that he thinks he can sit in judgment of others. He's so judgmental that not only does he point out the other person's shortcomings, but has the nerve to offer suggestions on how you can improve yourself so that you can be better for him. Who in the hell, but I digress. He's never once stopped to think about all the women he's dated have left him, including his ex-wife. If every woman he's ever dated left him, how in the world does this fool think it's everybody else with the problem?

Mr. Selfish did have some good qualities but the bad ones outweighed them overwhelmingly. Yes, he could cook, clean, and he was hard-working. He chipped in on the bills and made sure repairs on the house and cars were taken care of. Yes, I do like those qualities in a man, but I refuse to be reminded at every turn that he doesn't need me because he's an independent man. If that's the case, why was he with me then? Hell, I had to tell him to pack his independent shit and get his independent ass out my house. Yeah, you read right. His independent ass was living with me. Before he moved in with me, he lived with his cousin. Before his cousin, it was his last girlfriend.

Most men complain about independent women but do they realize that independent men can be just as bad or worse? When he continuously tells his woman he doesn't need her, and he can cook better than her, or he can do this or that better than her, he will soon find out he will be doing it without her and wondering why. He doesn't see that he did anything wrong. At least that's the thought that keeps them sleeping at night.

That Bitch Is Crazy

After 10 years of marriage, Mary put Bill out. He had to

go. Bill had gotten on her last nerve for the last time. She knew that she would struggle as a single parent trying to raise the kids by herself, but she was at her wit's end. She was sick and tired of being sick of his mess.

Bill came home in his usual fashion. He walked in the house, hugged her and the kids, and went to sit in his favorite chair. He looked around the living room and noticed the kids' toys all over the floor and started in on Mary. Never mind the fact Mary had worked a twelve hour day, took one child to ballet and the other to football practice, ran to the grocery store, picked them both up, and helped them with homework while trying to make dinner. She fed the kids, made sure they got their baths, and finally read bedtime stories before putting them to bed. This was a typical day for Mary.

After she finally got the kids down, she sat down to relax for a few minutes. She knew the living room was a mess and that she needed to straighten it up, but she was tired. She needed a few moments to get her second wind.

Bill, who happened to get off early for once, came home only to find his home in disarray. Little did he know, usually by the time he got home, Mary had already tidied up, but tonight he arrived home earlier.

As tired as Mary was, she still waited for him to get home from work because when he came in at 12:30 a.m., he would wake her up to talk because he wasn't sleepy yet. Sometimes, he would keep her up so long until she couldn't go back to sleep and then he would get in the bed, turn his back to her, and complain because she was watching television. That's a whole other issue.

He started in on Mary about the nasty house. He pointed out that she shouldn't have let the kids mess up the living room. He expressed his concern for her lack of parenting skills and the fact that she needed to manage her time better. All of this came at Mary after a stressful day she had, and it wasn't the first time. He could find fault with everything. Never once did he offer to help or assist in these matters.

Mary was usually the quiet type and non-confrontational. Generally speaking, she typically let things slide or would address them in a polite and calm manner. As usual, Bill never paid attention to what she had to say. Occasionally, he apologized just to pacify her but it was apparent he didn't mean it and he would do it again.

Mary finally exploded in a fit of rage. She had enough of his abuse. She snapped and let him have it with both barrels. She told him to get out. She stormed into their bedroom and began throwing his things outside. She even got her gun and told him to leave. Bill was horrified. He never expected her to act like that.

Once he was outside, she packed up everything that she

hadn't thrown out in garbage bags and put it on the curb. She called the police to make sure he left.

Bill came back the next day to find the locks changed. A few weeks later, divorce papers were served. He didn't know what happened. In his eyes, "the bitch was crazy." He was still in a state of shock. Selfish Bill was clearly blind to the fact that he caused this problem.

Chapter 5

The Workaholic

Now you really are going to be surprised by this one. Mr. Workaholic is the guy who works at least 16 hours per day. He is gone away from home working six of the seven days out of the week. When he *is* at home, he is so tired from working that he doesn't want to be bothered by the girlfriend/wife or kids. He will tolerate the kids a little while but not for very long. He is the hard-working brother who pays the bills. He really does take care of his family, financially. They don't want for anything. At least that's what he thinks.

From his perspective, he does what a man is supposed to do. His mate is happy to a certain degree. The reason she's not happy is because she has everything, except him. He is just as important to her as the money he is bringing in. He doesn't realize that he's leaving her alone. He is not giving her the most important part of the relationship... himself.

While his intentions are good, his methods are not.

Women love to spend quality time with their men. They don't have to always leave home or dress up for these things. She wants to know that she is special. He can't make her feel that way from work. She wants to cuddle, watch television, have a candlelight dinner for two, a picnic in the living room or just something.

I respected the fact that my man worked, but I was upset and disappointed because that was all he did. I really wanted to spend more quality time with him, but he was either too busy or too tired. He didn't have time for all of that, unless he wanted sex, in which case he could spare fifteen to thirty minutes for a quickie with no foreplay or cuddling.

This made me feel undesired or wanted. I felt like I was being used just for his needs mine weren't being met. You should know this crap wasn't about to last too long, married or not.

I began to feel lonely. I was tired of sitting at home alone and missing out on all of the fun because he was always working. I started hanging with my girlfriends, occasionally. It was all innocent fun because it gave me something to do besides sitting at home alone. We all know that things can turn around quickly even with the best intentions.

Too Busy to Help

Derrell was the typical workaholic with type A personality. On his off days, he simply worked from home. He would get up early, kiss his wife and kids, and leave for the day. By the time he came home, they were in bed. This was his routine. He had a great job at an architectural firm and was well compensated. However, he worked almost 70 hours per week, plus Saturdays and Sundays. He was never available to his family for anything. When he went to his kids' events, he worked on his phone and basically still missed it. He might as well have stayed at work, for all of the attention he gave.

Cindy, his wife, complained constantly about feeling like a single parent and being alone in their marriage. She often talked about needing help around the house and with the kids. She talked to him about his absence from their lives. His response was always the same—he was making sure they were provided for. She reminded him he was not the only person with an income and that he didn't have to work on his off days. She was willing to concede that much. However, he didn't agree and continued to work ridiculous hours.

The children were in high school. They participated in all types of academic and extracurricular activities, including basketball, track, baseball, cheerleading, debate team, and the academic bowl team. They were honor students who were in the top of their respective classes. They were model students who longed for their father to be a part of their activities more, especially the sports, but Derrell was always too busy.

Over the years, Cindy began to get tired of being lonely. She felt that if she was going to be a single parent then that's exactly what she should be. She never thought of cheating on Derrell because she loved him dearly, but there was James.

James was too fine for words. He often flirted with Cindy at work. She politely reminded him she was married. James was considered to be the catch of the century. All the women in the office wanted him, but he wanted Cindy. For months, he continuously tried to make his presence known by inviting her to lunch, bringing her flowers and candy. No one was the wiser because she was married. Coworkers naturally assumed the items came from her husband.

One day, while at work, Cindy broke down and cried. She thought she was alone in the lounge but as she was crying, James made his presence known. He didn't say anything. He simply handed her some tissue and sat beside her. He gave her the shoulder she needed to cry on. He allowed her to fall completely apart in his presence. James didn't know what to say to comfort her so he made no verbal attempt. A few minutes after Cindy's break down, James reminded her that they both needed to return to work. He helped to steady her as she rose to stand. He opened his arms to offer her a friendly hug. She melted in his embrace as his body fit hers like a glove. She apologized for her unprofessional behavior and thanked him dearly for being there.

When Cindy got off work, she went through her usual paces of the day but waited for Derrell to come home from work. She really needed to talk to him. By the time he got home, he was dog-tired and didn't want to be bothered. She pleaded with him because she was scared. The one thing that scared her was the development of feelings for James. Somehow, she knew that if things didn't get better at home, something was going to happen. She wasn't looking to make anything happen, but when she was in James' arms for that hug, it felt so good.

Cindy began to fantasize about James. At first, she thought it was because she was needy and he had been there for her, but now she wasn't so sure. James was a dream. He became her friend, confidante, strength, and comforter. Was it possible she was falling in love with him? No, she was married. She had a hard-working husband who loved her and their kids.

James invited her over for drinks or coffee many times

but she always turned him down because of her marriage and loyalty to her family. However, he always left the door open to the possibilities. Finally, she walked through that open door. She was tired of being ignored. She eventually took the kids and moved out. She served Derrell with divorce papers.

Derrell was devastated. He couldn't understand why she wanted a divorce. He searched high and low for her. He didn't want to go to her job but that was the only location where she was guaranteed to be. When he reached the floor where she worked, he saw her and James. That's when he realized that she needed him but he was never available. Now he was free to work all he wanted.

Chapter 6

Mr. Insecure

The insecure man is so damn smothering. He wants to control every aspect of your life, especially your friendships. He even had the nerve to tell me, "Don't let her shit rub off on you." This was because I wouldn't end my friendship with someone I had known for thirty years. This asinine fool must have been out of his mind to think I would leave my friend just because she didn't fall for his bull. He didn't like the fact that I could see right through him.

Mr. Insecure is jealous and manipulative. He will often accuse you of cheating just because you have male friends. Hell, I have male friends because sometimes females can be catty, jealous, and full of drama. Sorry ladies, but you know this is true. I ain't got no time for that bullshit.

He looks for your constant reassurance that he was and is the "one." When he feels your attention is somewhere else, he may criticize your appearance or any area that he feels you are vulnerable. He is seriously co-dependent on you. If he cannot mentally control you, he will sometimes resort to physical abuse followed by an apology and gifts.

I never will be the type to take an ass whipping so he only got that one chance to seriously fuck up. This behavior is usually attributed to lack of confidence in oneself. There was something about him that he felt he could not do, usually sexual insecurity, so it manifested itself as dominant and controlling.

If you remember the story of Ike and Tina Turner, "What's Love Got to Do with It," Ike mentally controlled Tina. He began to physically abuse her. Insecure men often have a need to control their environment. This is the security blanket they use to feel better about themselves. Ultimately, their need to control causes more harm than good. In this case, he is lucky that he was able to leave standing.

I Love Her Too Much

Mike was Mr. Insecure. He loved his woman, Shana, with all of his heart or at least that's what she was supposed to think. He gave her everything she wanted, as long as she obeyed him. However, he never seemed to realize that his rules were ridiculous. For example, she couldn't speak to other men, especially if he was around to see it, even if there were other women in the group. Another one was that she couldn't associate with her friends who were single or not in a relationship. Finally, she could only go out if he knew where, when, and how long she was going to be out, along with who she going out with. It was ludicrous. His reign over her was stifling. She couldn't breathe without him wanting to know why she exhaled. He was still legally married so technically he was cheating on his wife with Shana.

On Saturday, she ran into her friends, Renita and Monica, at a baseball park. All of them had children who played baseball. Shana and the others were standing and socializing when Renita's brother walked up and spoke to the group. This was something he always did. He never tried to date any of his sister's friends.

Mike saw them talking and immediately called Shana on her cell phone. He was a few feet away and could have come over to join the conversation. Instead, he told her to leave the group and return to him. Upon her return, he privately cursed her out and made her stay away from the group for the rest of the day. She later told Monica why she had to leave. When Monica asked her why she put up with his type of control, she said it was because of the kids. It was clear there was fear in her eyes. She was unquestionably scared of what Mike might do.

Monica and Shana had been friends for several years. Shana often confided in Monica about the things Mike had done to her in the past. He had beaten up on her a few times and they also fought verbally. Occasionally, she showed up with fresh bruises on various parts of her body. Of course, she had a plausible story for how they got there. Monica was the only one who knew what was going on, but the other women speculated about it.

For many years, she tolerated his abuse. This also included the fact she often discovered he was cheating on her with other women. She even followed him to the other women's houses and knocked on their doors to get him out.

While he was doing all of his dirt, he had the nerve to tell her he loved her. He used her only weakness, the children, so he manipulated them. Whenever she left him to start a new life for her and the kids, he would tell the kids how much he missed and loved his family. He laid the guilt on so heavily to their children that they would beg Shana to forgive him so that they could stay together as a family. Each and every time this happened, she broke down and went back to him. He even proposed to her in a very public party in front of their friends to demonstrate his love for her. All the while, he was still seeing another woman.

Shana accepted his proposal, hoping he would be for real this time. This was the continuous cycle for many years until the children were old enough to realize what was going on.

By the time the children were teens, they realized their dad was not right in the way he treated their mother. They began to tell her to leave him and not put up with his mess and abuse anymore. Shana couldn't believe what she was hearing from her own children, but she knew then it was time to leave.

She found a place for her and the children. Each weekend, without Mike knowing, Shana packed clothes and belongings and little by little took them to the new place. She created the illusion that everything was alright between them. Finally, she took the children and moved while he was out of town with another woman. By the time Mike found out she was gone, it was too late.

This was the end of the road for Mr. Insecure. His manipulations were over. He couldn't control Shana or the kids any longer.

Chapter 7

The Gossip - I Heard What "They said" About You

For me, the worst thing a man can do is tell me what a friend or ex said about me. How would they feel if their woman went behind their back and checked their background with people they have had negative encounters with or people who never really got to know them? For him to do this to me was an insult. Furthermore, he ruined any attempt to truly get to know me for himself. He prejudiced his own mind without realizing it. Not only that, he has no idea if what he was told about me is true. This subsequently holds him back from allowing himself to be open-minded. As far as I'm concerned, he can kick rocks.

Ladies, when you hear tales from people, there are things we need to consider. First, consider the source. Second, has the person with the information had a relationship with this man? What type of relationship did they have? Why did the relationship end or change? Third, is the person talking truthful? Are you getting the full story about what happened? Fourth, why are they telling me this information? What's their motivation? Why is this person suddenly voluntarily sharing information? How is he going to approach me to discuss the information that he's heard or is he going to discuss it at all?

Please understand when someone brings up the subject of what "they" had to say about me, don't be surprised when they're no longer my mate anymore. I am not going to put up with it, I can assure you. Furthermore, you wouldn't either. You wouldn't like or appreciate it one little bit. You'd be pissed too. I know. Next, see how one gossiping ass man got what he deserved.

She Got Tired

As luck would have it, Dina met Stacy on social media. The conversations they had started through a mutual friend over football. Although they went to the same high school and lived in the same city, they had never previously met. They knew a lot of the same people but somehow never encountered each other.

As time progressed, their conversations went to the inbox and eventually to the telephone. Stacy decided since the conversations were so good, they should meet in person.

He called Dina and asked her out. Dina was reluctant to see him alone since they really didn't know each other. She invited her friend along and asked him to invite a friend too. The four of them met at Applebee's and had a wonderful time. Dina and Stacy began dating and building a relationship. They shared some of the same values and expectations. He took her to meet his adult kids and he met hers. This seemed to be a promising situation for them both.

After a few months of dating, Stacy disappeared for about three weeks. He didn't call or go to see Dina. She was curious about what happened but figured he'd call when he was ready to talk. During that three-week period, Dina met a guy named Ricky. He asked her out on dates but she told him she couldn't because of her uncertain situation with Stacy. He understood but continued his pursuit of her without pressure.

During his disappearance, Stacy contacted people he knew that could possibly know Dina. He asked about her, her family, financial status, and reputation. The problem was he asked people that she had not dealt with for years or they were acquaintances she only spoke to in passing. Stacy had no idea the information he got was false, but there was no one who could give him any real truth in the people that he chose to question.

Dina had always been a private person. She had very

few friends that met her boyfriends prior to them being in a serious relationship. So even her friends knew only a little.

Upon his return, Stacy decided to go see Dina. By this time, she had been out with Ricky, platonically, several times. She did, however, tell Ricky about Stacy so that there would be no misunderstanding. Ricky completely understood her situation and told her that they could be friends. Of course, this didn't stop Ricky from trying to become more than her friend at every chance. Ricky made his point of view very clear even though he was rebuffed. He decided to wait it out because he had a feeling, based on Dina, things were about to change.

Stacy, on the other hand, was deciding how he would "play" the situation with Dina without realizing he had already lost her attention. His tactics simply pushed her farther away. He created unnecessary arguments so he could point out her shortcomings. He stood her up on dates and lied about why. He did everything he could to try to break her down. Little did he know that in the midst of his attempts, Ricky was there to help her. Stacy's behavior bordered on abuse. He did everything he could to try to break Dina's self-esteem. He went so far as to start dating someone else but tried to hide it from Dina. He didn't know that she had already overheard him on the phone talking to the other woman. Dina was way ahead of his game.

After a few weeks of this behavior, Dina was fed up and fired up. She went on a natural warpath. She told Stacy about himself in the midst of a heated argument. That's when the grits hit the fan!

He shouted at her with the information that he had gathered behind her back. He told her everything *they* told him. He admitted that was why his behavior towards her changed.

After that, Dina dismissed him completely. She told him to get the fuck out of her house. Stacy wanted to talk rationally. He begged, pleaded, and tried to work it out, but Dina was done. She wasn't interested in talking, listening, or working things out. She cut off all forms of communication with him. She blocked his number from her phone and gave his tag number to the security officer just in case he thought about dropping by her apartment unannounced.

In retrospect, she could have done things differently, but for him to attach her name to gossip from people that didn't know her was the final straw. He believed rumors and lies from weak sources and threw that in her face. She heard things about him and could gage people's reactions when they found out who she was dating. Never had it occurred to her to do a background check on him and treat him like what she'd heard. What kind of crap was that!

Chapter 8

The Whining Ass

Most women really hate meeting the whining ass man. I know I do. He's the one who wants to be "the man" but can't handle the fact that you're financially independent. He's always complaining because he feels insecure because of your income. He whines and complains so much until it becomes aggravating and a major turnoff. Most men would call a woman like this a nag. Keep in mind that you never once complained about his income or financial status. This is all in his damn head. If I had a problem with his income, I didn't have to date him to begin with. Furthermore, most independent women aren't looking for a father. We're looking for a companion, friend, lover, and confidante. The rest is irrelevant. The only person who feels inadequate is him.

The other type of whining ass man is the one who has had bad experiences in his past relationships and can't seem to get over it. He meets a good woman but can't appreciate her because he's too busy living in his past. He complains about how he's been treated, people who used him for his money, those that mistreated him because he loved them, those that took advantage of his kindness (not necessarily relationships). While I will try to be understanding at first, there comes a point when I say, *"You can have your pity party by yourself. It's time for you to move on to something new and better. You can be with me or someone else, but get a grip."* Here's how another one bites the dust:

He Pushed Her Away

Tim saw Michelle walking down the aisle at church and his mouth fell open. He was literally speechless. He had forgotten that he was working security and was supposed to be watching the crowd. All he saw was her. She was an angel, or at least that's what he thought. He admired her for months without actually approaching her because he thought she was out of his league. In an effort to size her up, he observed who she spoke to at church, who she socialized with, and how she treated people. Tim was vigilant in his observations.

Tim finally got the nerve to ask Michelle for her phone number. She was happy to give him her number because she was attracted to him also.

As they became acquainted with each other, Michelle noticed that Tim kept giving her mixed signals. One minute he seemed like he was falling for her, then the next minute he acted like he didn't care one way or the other. These mixed signals were confusing and frustrating. She was growing tired of it and was becoming disinterested.

Haunted by his past, Tim couldn't believe that he had finally met the woman of his dreams. He continuously did unexplainable things like not communicating with her, shutting her out, and being moody. He was waiting for her to turn into this evil person, to begin to try to use him for something. He had convinced himself that she was just too good to be true, and in some ways, she was.

Like Tim, Michelle had been married before. She knew what it took to be a Proverbs 31 woman and she lived by that standard. She was a praying, dependable, trustworthy friend with no ulterior motive. The thing Tim didn't realize is that she was the same with everyone, not just him. She was the type of friend that prayed for and with you. She would join your fast and intercede on your behalf. She was a *real* friend.

Michelle really began to like Tim and she could see that he had a good heart. She could also see that he had some unresolved issues which contributed to his moody behavior. She prayed about their relationship and decided to just love

Tim. She believed he needed to be loved genuinely. She treated him like a king; cooking, honoring, respecting, and doing those things that most men appreciate. She actually loved him. She let him know he was not alone and that everyone wasn't out to get over on him.

Tim reveled in her treatment but still showed signs of reluctance, but Michelle never wavered. Tim began to allow his walls to finally fall. Although very guarded, he couldn't help but love her and the way she made him feel. Now he treated her very well and did things to reciprocate the treatment he received from her. He let her know how special she was to him. One only needed to look at the way he stared at her to see the love he was trying unsuccessfully to hide.

After nine months of dating, the ultimate test came when Tim's ex-wife came to his job at the church, where she knew he would be working security, and Michelle would be for service. Tim had not initially seen his ex until he was about to get off. She walked up to him in an unusually flirtatious mode and spoke. She batted her eyes and tried to hug him. Tim was shocked she showed up on his job, flirting with him as if they had something going. He took a step back because Michelle was there and he had no idea of how to explain the situation. He didn't know if she had seen this incident. He didn't know if she would be jealous. His mind was inundated with all types of questions and thoughts. What should he do about this? Apparently, his ex-wife had heard that he was seeing someone and being the drama queen that she is decided to interfere as usual and be messy.

Michelle, totally unaware of the situation, saw him standing at his duty post and walked up in the usual manner and spoke. He gave her an uninviting half hello. Michelle stepped back, looked at him, and asked him what was wrong. He nervously twitched and shuffled from one foot to the other. He kept peeping over his shoulder as if someone was watching. She asked him a second time but still got no real answer. Michelle wasn't the type to jump to conclusions so she sat down and patiently waited for Tim to come tell her what was bothering him. After a few minutes, Tim got up the nerve to tell Michelle about his ex-wife showing up at his work.

Once Tim revealed the truth to Michelle, she said, "Oh, well that's fine." She was a little upset but she knew that his job was not the place to discuss the matter. She let him know they could talk about it later and gave him his usual hug and smile. Talk about waiting to exhale, Tim took the deepest breath ever. He was relieved to know that Michelle understood enough to be willing to talk and not judge.

Michelle had her own questions about his ex-wife and her motives. She wanted to know if Tim had encouraged this behavior in any way. Michelle went home and began to ponder the situation. She talked to her sister about the entire incident.

Sisters are amazing sometimes. Her sister listened attentively and began to put herself in the same scenario. She advised Michelle to think of the situation in reverse and to examine the motives of the ex-wife. She pointed out that the ex-wife's intentions were to create drama. She also reminded Michelle that Tim was placed in an awkward position and probably didn't know how to handle it Michelle's sister advised her not to jump to any conclusions and be willing to listen openly.

Michelle calmed down and took time to pray as she always did in stressful situations. She decided to listen to her sister and give Tim a chance to communicate. It was the best decision she could have made.

Tim told Michelle he did not invite his ex-wife to his job. She just showed up. Michelle concluded that Tim's ex-wife was up to no good. Tim, on the other hand, took things more personally. He immediately built a wall back up and shut everyone out again, including Michelle. For Michelle, this was the final straw, and she decided to let him go. Heartbroken and disappointed as she was, he gave her no alternative. She walked away from Tim because he kept living and whining about his past.

Although Tim and Michelle remained friends, he realized that the only thing that hurt his relationship was his past. He regretted that he lost Michelle because of his moody ways. He finally made up in his mind that the next time he met someone like Michelle, he wouldn't allow his past to interfere with his future.

Chapter 9

The Arrogant Ass

These motherfuckers make me sick. They think they are God's gift to the world. They truly believe they have it going on. They don't realize how far from the truth they are. If they are all that they think they are, why can't they keep a woman? I'll tell you the answer to that question. Nobody can love their perfect ass as much as they do. The problem is they haven't looked in a mirror lately. You see, they don't have it all together like they think they do. This pitiful piece of crap has the nerve to think that all women want him.

Once when I was at work, this arrogant ass had the audacity to tell some of our co-workers that I wanted him. When someone asked me about it, I was confused. I hadn't done anything nor said anything to elicit this comment. We had previously spent time laughing and talking to each other but nothing else. I simply thought it was workplace camaraderie. Nothing about the conversation suggested I liked him. As a matter of fact, he did almost all of the talking about the Bible. Most of that time, I was laughing because he was a comedian and his jokes were hilarious. The next day, I was blindsided about my "flirting" with him by a mutual friend. Damn! He was really on his own "sac." Never once had I thought about him in that manner. Besides, I keep my money and my honey in two separate places. Rule number one has always been *never shit and eat in the same place at the same time.*

Most people see this arrogance and dismiss it because they know the truth. People look beyond what they think they have going on and try to see the real person underneath all of the bullshit. Too bad they won't do the same for others. They come up with their ideal female in their heads. In reality, they can't pull that kind of female even if they tried, not for real. Just a Note: Beyoncé won't date Buddha.

They treat you according to how you look, how much money they think you have, and the car you drive. These men don't think about the fact they had to buy a used, five to ten year old BMW or Mercedes and you bought a brand new Honda. They look for superficial exteriors that don't matter because they think they have an image to uphold. In reality, nobody gives a shit about that but them. Consequently, they miss out on good people who aren't trying to use them.

They always end up with the same type of people, "gold diggers," then have the nerve to wonder why. **They need to get their heads out of their asses and look at the heart of people!**

He Lost Proverbs 31 for Jezebel

Lee met Nancy when they were in middle school. They lived in neighboring neighborhoods and played together as kids. As a matter of fact, Lee's sister was friends with Nancy. They hadn't seen each other in over 30 years after Nancy moved and they went to different schools. Thanks to social media, they reconnected. The communication was so good that after four months of communicating, they decided to meet in person. They both loved sports, travel, fine dining, and family. They shared some of their life's highs and lows and had begun to build a level of trust and respect for one another.

Lee was tall, tan, and handsome. He was nicely built but not the "stripper type of fine" and had a great job. He was a churchgoing, hard-working man who was divorced with grown kids. He drove a nice car and had a nice home. One would think that a man with these qualities was a pretty good catch. However, the truth would show up.

Nancy was a well-dressed, beautiful, plus-sized, sales

agent. When she talked to Lee, she never lied to him about her size. She informed him of her battle with weight loss and the fact that she was still working on herself physically. Lee claimed that it didn't matter but in reality, it did.

The blind date was set for them to meet. Nancy arrived at the meeting location where she and Lee had designated. When he arrived and saw her face, he smiled. She returned the smile. He got out of his car and walked over to hers and opened the door. When she stepped out of the car, he gave her an appropriate hug and they began to talk. The conversation lasted hours. They walked around the park and had a picnic lunch by the pond.

Lee pulled out a book of poetry he had written over the years and shared some of his writing. She was quite impressed with his work and encouraged him to get it published. Since he had shared something so personal with her, she felt confident that maybe things would just get better. She was wrong.

In the next few weeks, Lee stopped calling or making gestures in her direction. When she attempted to contact him, she could tell he was either avoiding her or lying to her. He stood her up a couple of times. By now, Nancy was sure Tim had decided not to date her. However, his cowardly ass couldn't admit to himself or her that it was because of her body size. His arrogant ass was so shallow that he couldn't see pass her size enough to think about how much fun they had previously. Nancy had seen this type of behavior before, so she recognized it right off. Nancy simply walked away from Lee without a second thought.

A couple of years later, Nancy was out with the girls at a party. She saw Lee and remembered him right off. Lee, on the other hand, did not know that she had finally won her battle of the bulge, and he did not recognize Nancy at all. As she danced with her friends and enjoyed the party, Lee admired her from afar. Finally, he waited for her to be alone at the table to make his move. This was his chance to step to her. As he approached Nancy, she sat sipping her margarita.

Lee got to her table and asked, "Is this seat taken?"

"No."

"Do you mind if I join you?"

"That would be fine."

"I'm Lee."

"Hi." Nancy chose not to tell him her name right then. She wanted to savor the moment for the right occasion. They chatted for a brief moment. As the conversation continued, his face began to show signs of confusion or bewilderment. Right about the time things were becoming clear to him as to who she might be, she introduced herself and then told him goodbye. Lee was in utter shock! He couldn't believe how good she looked. Furthermore, he couldn't believe she politely dismissed him in the same manner that he had done.

Note: What goes around will definitely come back around.

Chapter 10

Mr. Manipulator

Ladies, you know we've all seen this guy. He's the one who tries to become your every wish and dream come true. He becomes your best friend, your lover, your "ride or die." He makes you feel like he is your everything and you can't live without him. He may even stoop so far as to get you pregnant just so he can be a part of your life. He might even tell you he will commit suicide if he can't be with you. However, he tries to make you feel like he is doing you a favor by spending time with you. He uses emotion, guilt, and any other method to keep you where he can manipulate you. Usually, he's a lot older than you, gives you some experiences that you have never had, and blows your mind.

At first, every time you think of him, you get that warm, wet feeling all over. You must be careful of this one because he looks for your vulnerabilities and plays on them. He's looking for an angle where he can come up.

This man is the biggest liar in the world. The only problem is he makes you fall so in love with him that you overlook his lies and deceptions. You ignore everyone and everything. You even ignore the red lights that God Himself shows you. He has you so bamboozled that you even defy your parents and people you love and respect just for him. How many of us have fallen into this category? Check out this story….

So Young, So Naïve

Nancy was a young virgin who had lived a sheltered life. Her parents made sure she had the best of everything they could provide. She was smart, attractive, and naïve. She was in college before she had her first real boyfriend. He moved into her apartment and became an abusive man who misused her and treated her like crap. He didn't start out treating her like that. He was smart enough to calculate and maneuver his way into her heart. He became her worse nightmare. It took her quite some time to end the relationship and gather her senses to move forward with her life.

However, she jumped straight out of the fire into the frying pan. She met Lonny at a club one night where he was working security. He was cute and fine. He paid attention to her. He treated her like she had never been treated before.

He was so much better than her previous abusive boyfriend. As a matter of fact, he wiped her tears and listened as she shared with him about the experiences from her last relationship. He was there for her. Lonny seemed to be the ideal man. I say *seemed* to be ideal. He gave her everything she needed emotionally at that time to make her feel like he was "the" man.

He came home with her to meet her family. He acted as though he was so in love with Nancy. He asked her dad if he could have her hand in marriage. He got her pregnant before the wedding, and they had a daughter.

After the birth of their child, Nancy decided she wanted to move, get a job in her hometown, and be closer to her parents. Now that she had graduated with her second master's degree, she felt she was finally qualified to get the job she wanted at the zoo as a veterinarian. Lonny moved with her. He said she needed him and he wanted to be a father to their child. While some might see this as noble and responsible, the truth was far from that.

He started telling her, "I gave up everything to come here to be with you," especially when they were having an argument. That's the guilt he made sure he laid on her as often as he could. He even had her saying it.

Truths began to reveal themselves that had been hidden previously from her parents. First, he had four other children that he didn't take care of. Second, he had an extensive criminal history. Third, his relationship with his mother and family was not a good one. Fourth, he was at least ten or more years older than her. And finally, he was the biggest liar that anyone had ever met because he was addicted to cocaine and not even Nancy knew that. All of this information eventually came out while they were living with her parents.

When Nancy was confronted with this information, she chose not to see the truth. Her parents and friends had met and sized up her fiancé. They began to see he was an opportunist, a liar, and a manipulator.

Lonny convinced Nancy of his love for her and how they needed to be together. She was so in love that she was "swimming in the Kool-Aid." She had completely blinded herself to the fact he was not the man for her.

He almost killed her and their daughter and gave some sorry excuse to her. She bought it hook, line, and sinker. Her parents told her of his lies, lack of concern while she was in the hospital, and the fact that they caught him in numerous lies.

At 6:30 a.m. Tina's phone rang. "Hello."

It was Lonny. "Hey, big sis. Can I come over? I need to talk. It's important."

"Yes, come over." Tina got out of bed and got dressed

because at that hour, she knew that whatever he needed to talk to her about had to be extremely important. About twenty minutes later, there was a knock at the door.

"Hi, what's going on?" asked Tina.

"Man, I can't believe how Nancy's dad just got down on me."

"What do you mean? Why would he go off on you? He wouldn't just go off for no reason. Maybe you need to start from the beginning." Keep in mind, Tina had been friends with Nancy's family, the Potters, for over twenty years. She watched Nancy grow up. No one could tell her anything negative about the Potters without her having some questions.

"Nancy is in the hospital. She got sick at work and I had to rush her to the emergency room. She was immediately sent to surgery. Apparently, her appendix ruptured. I called Mr. and Mrs. Potter to let them know. Mr. Potter came to the emergency room with us and Mrs. Potter stayed home with our daughter.

"What? Hospital? Why didn't anyone call me before now?" Tina began to panic because this was serious. She needed to get the whole story so she backed off with her questions to wait for the rest of the information.

"Nancy collapsed on the floor in the ladies' room."

"I still don't get why Mr. Potter went off on you." She

was still perplexed.

"Well, while we were at the hospital Mr. Potter was asking questions about what happened. I answered him as best as I could, but he was tripping. He blamed me for her being in the hospital. It wasn't my fault. I tried to get her to go see the doctor weeks ago but she wouldn't because we have no insurance."

"If you knew she wasn't feeling well, why didn't you tell her mother you thought something was wrong? Her mother would have forced her to go."

"She didn't want her folks to know. I respected her wishes."

"You jackass! Do you realize someone being sick for over two weeks is more than a virus and requires medical attention? Why didn't you come to me? I would have done something. That's why Mr. Potter got in your ass! You were careless and irresponsible!"

Tina was fuming inside because this idiot had put Nancy in danger. She told Lonny to relax and take a nap on the sofa and when he got up, they would both go back to the hospital to see about Nancy. But there was something about this story that didn't sound right. Mr. Potter never lost his cool, no matter how difficult the situation so Tina was suspicious. She felt there was something missing.

When Lonny woke up, Tina suggested he go home and

change clothes. He also needed to get the baby so that Mrs. Potter could get to the hospital. In the meantime, Tina got ready to go to the hospital herself.

When Tina arrived at the hospital, she saw Mr. and Mrs. Potter. They embraced, which was their usual custom. "Okay, y'all I had a visitor this morning. Lonny came by very upset and said you got down on him. What's going on?"

Mr. Potter said, "You're damn right I got down on him! My child was in surgery fighting for her life and I'm pacing the floor waiting for some news and his sorry ass was asleep! He wasn't concerned in the least about her. The doctor said the surgery was supposed to take about twenty minutes. Over two hours passed and we hadn't heard anything. I was praying for my child's life and he was sleep!"

"Oh my, why did it take so long? Were there complications in the surgery?"

"I woke him up after the doctor came in to let us know what happened. When I tried to get the details about the cause of the surgery, he acted like it wasn't a big deal and that I shouldn't overreact."

"Shouldn't overreact? What the hell?"

"Exactly my point. He took out his phone and began to play video games while I was trying to have a conversation with him. I wanted to throw that phone against a wall, and him too! He's lucky I didn't.'"

Nancy recovered just fine, and was soon discharged. Now it was time for that talk. It was going to be a difficult conversation between Nancy and her parents. They informed her of everything that occurred between her dad and Lonny while she was in surgery. She listened to the concerns of her parents but made no decisions about her future or Lonny. She was heartbroken and confused and no doubt very vulnerable. She needed to talk to Lonny about the accusations leveled against him. She couldn't fathom any of this being true, but her parents never lied to her.

However, with every beat of her heart, she listened to Lonny. It didn't matter what anyone else said. She turned to Tina to talk about the issues concerning her parents and fiancé. Her friend began to pray and look for the wisdom necessary to discuss the situation at hand.

Tina began to speak to Nancy and ask her some significant questions that should have opened Nancy's eyes, but again it didn't. Tina asked Nancy to take a piece of notebook paper and write down Lonny's good attributes and contributions to her life. On the other side, she was to write down the bad things. Lonny saw Nancy working on this project, and separated Nancy and Tina.

Tina didn't know what he said or did, but one thing she did know was she and Nancy didn't talk or hang out like they used to and she never got that project back. They are still friends but they do not get to see each other very much anymore and definitely not alone; just the girls. He always managed to interfere with their plans. Poor Nancy still didn't seem to be aware of his manipulations.

Tina and Nancy's parents chose not to get involved any further. They prayed for her because they knew she would eventually learn what they had seen all along.

This ongoing saga has yet to end. Only time will tell how Nancy's life turns out. As of right now, she's still planning on marrying his trifling butt.

Chapter 11

Mr. Lazy "Mama's Little Man"

Ladies, we all know that one man who is tied up into his mom and all the things that she has done to ruin him for any quality female. He is spoiled, selfish, and almost completely intolerable. He has the nerve to think we are supposed to treat him like his mother does. I don't think so! Just because his mama took care of him like he was a baby for 35 years, doesn't mean that I'm going to do it.

It is not my responsibility to take care of a grown ass man because he is either too trifling or too lazy to do it himself. He will not live in my house and not work. Even the Bible says, "The man that doesn't work, doesn't eat." If he thinks for one minute he is going to lay up in my house and sleep, eat my food, watch TV, and wear my bedroom slippers while I go to work all day, he'd better think again. And a part-time job won't cut it. Ain't nothing going on but the mortgage up in here.

Furthermore, every time there is a situation between this man and his woman, he has to call his mother to "tell" on her like she's his little sister. Does he think his mother is going to tell his woman what to do or how to live her life? Does he think his woman has to "obey" his mother? He looks for his mother to give him advice for living with his woman. This is never a good idea because his mother isn't in the household nor does she pay the bills there. His mother gives terrible advice on how he should "handle" his woman and then blames the woman for why things are all wrong.

I'm not hating on men, but some of them give real men a bad name and a wrong meaning. Don't get me wrong, certain circumstances may prevent him from working but that's not who I'm talking about. I'm referring to the lazy, able-bodied man who expects his woman to be the man he thinks he is and has the nerve to say with a straight face that he is a grown ass man.

You're Not Dating Your Mama

Javon was the apple of his mother's eye. She gave him the best of everything. He loved the way she cooked and did his laundry. Occasionally, she brought him breakfast in his room. Javon grew up spoiled. He was not held accountable nor made to be responsible throughout his entire life. Poor Javon couldn't even turn in his own school projects. His mom would bring them to the school for him after she completed them. While his mother thought she was doing what was best for him, she had no real clue that she was hurting him in the long run.

Javon graduated from high school, thanks to his mom, but had no future plans or aspirations. He simply drifted with the wind. He had no idea what he wanted to be or do. He changed jobs like most people changed clothes. If there was something that he didn't like about the job, he simply quit. Since he had no bills, in his mind, he thought he could just get another job. However, Javon had a son that was a year old. One would think he would have to pay child support, pick up his child for the weekend to spend time with him, and buy clothes. You know the usual stuff a parent is supposed to do. Nope! Good old Mom was there to do all of that.

Finally, one beautiful autumn day, Javon met Tosha. Tosha was gorgeous in his eyes. She was his Beyonce. However, she was what he called *high maintenance*. She kept her appearance immaculate, her clothing impeccable, and her shoes didn't come from some bargain basement sale. She was a pharmaceutical sales representative that made well over $80,000 a year. His broke ass wanted her.

Are you serious? Did he really think she would give him the time of day? He knew that he didn't stand a chance unless he got himself together. He played it cool with Tosha by just being friends.

Javon had never really been responsible before and had no clue as to what it took because his mom took care of everything for him. She did his laundry, paid his child support, took care of his son when he came over, and cooked his meals. He didn't have to clean his room or make his bed. Poor thing, seems like he had to ask his mom if he needed to think or not. How in the world would he stand a chance at getting next to Tosha?

He began to ask Tosha about her interests in men. Of course, his mom told him the type of information to ask that would help him. One would have thought he was a special education student. He was pitiful.

Tosha was attracted to Javon but she was cautious about him because she could clearly see that cute was the only thing there. She knew that he was financially challenged but felt that if she encouraged him and helped him find a job, he would step up. She asked him for a copy of his resume; he had to get it from his mom. She helped him to edit and correct his resume to make it presentable so that he might stand a chance. Ultimately, Javon found a job, thanks to Tosha. He still had not approached her about dating because he knew that it would take more than just a job.

Tosha encouraged him to become more independent by moving out into his own place.

"Hey, Javon, don't you think you need to move out of your mother's house?"

"Why?"

"Because you're a grown ass man living with your mommy," she mocked.

"I don't see why I should move. Besides, she doesn't want me to move out."

"So, you're scared to move out on your own? Why? Mommy not there to tuck you in at night?"

"Well, since you mentioned it. I'll consider what you're saying. Let me think about it." He really meant, "Let me ask my mom for permission."

Javon didn't see a need to move and his mother didn't want to be alone. Mind you, she was in her late forties and very attractive. If Javon wasn't in the picture, she probably could get a life or a man of her own. Javon knew that moving out would mean he couldn't spend his money like he wanted. Paying bills would stop him from being "big baller, shot caller." If he stayed with his mother, he wouldn't have to worry about that.

Javon was in a quandary because he wanted to get with Tosha but he didn't want to disappoint his mother. On the other hand, he had already surmised that if he didn't move into his own place, he wouldn't stand a chance in getting Tosha.

Finally, Javon decided it was time to make his move on Tosha. They went out on a romantic date and he treated her like a queen. Of course, she responded in kind so he felt like a king.

"Hey, Tosha, would you like to hang out with me on Friday? I want to go to that new Jamaican restaurant on 4th Street."

"Sure. I'm free on Friday."

After a few years of dating, Javon practically moved in with Tosha. He spent almost every night with her, but he had to leave every morning before she got ready for work. It was as if he lived there in a way, except he didn't have a key. "What's a brother got to do to get a key up in here?"

"Say 'I do' in front of a preacher and the mortgage is $1100 per month."

"I do and $1100? That's kind of steep, don't you think?"

"You asked what it would take."

"Is that why you make me leave before the sun comes up every time I try to spend the night?"

"Yes, you don't live here. You live with your mommy."

"Okay, so why you got to keep bringing that up?"

"Has the situation changed?"

Silence.

He really wanted a key but Tosha made it perfectly clear that without the "I do," he did not live in her house. He talked extensively with his mother about his relationship with Tosha. She knew every detail of every part of their relationship as if she was a part of it too. He even mentioned to his mom that he was thinking about marrying Tosha. He truly believed that she was the one for him.

He decided to bring Tosha around more so that his mother could get to know her better and get her approval. It was essential to Javon that his women like each other.

As Tosha began to spend more time around Javon and his family, she discovered there were some things that she didn't know about him. She actually had no clue as to who he really was because of the secrets. This was problem number one; hidden truth. She began to interact with his mother only to find out his mother knew way too many intimate details about their relationship. Furthermore, his mother took for granted that Tosha was aware of the fact their relationship was no secret.

Tosha wondered if he had more secrets, like kids, etc. that she didn't know about. All of this began to wear on Tosha. She became more and more irritated with the lies, half-truths, and secrets.

Tosha and Javon began to argue often and the discord

in their relationship only grew because his mom would call Tosha to discuss the problems in their relationship. Tosha felt like she might as well have been dating his mother instead of him. At least, she would have been hearing the truth up front instead of after the fact. She lost all trust in him. She began to lose respect for Javon as a man because all of his solutions to their problems came from his mother and not him. Finally, Tosha got tired of dating Javon and his mother so she dismissed him with a quickness.

Chapter 12

The Pretender

I don't know what this man is about. He's the one who claims he has it going on. He brags about everything, including his sexual prowess. He volunteers information you didn't ask for. Why? Girl, now we all know that braggers are a total waste of time. They are all talk or don't quite tell the real truth. They think they can impress you with what they have all while not realizing that you don't even care about any of the crap he's feeding you. For most of us, it's a major turn off or it makes us go into "put up or shut up mode." I'm not sure if the pretender or the arrogant ass is worse.

This fool thinks that making false promises and telling lies will make you do whatever he wants. That's ridiculous! First of all, only gold diggers are looking for sugar daddies. A real woman is not interested in a man's money because she has her own. She's a boss chick in her own right. As far as the sex goes, generally speaking, a real man doesn't brag about what he has or what he can do in bed. He will simply wait until the opportunity presents itself and then handle things like he needs to. We all know that if he's talking, keep it moving because we more than likely will be disappointed either in the performance or equipment. Here is the rundown on the pretender.

The "Rolly Polly" Fiasco

Dexter called his friend, Paul, and asked him if he knew of any single females that would be interested in dating. Paul reluctantly said that he would see if a friend was available. Paul called Kisha and asked her if she was seeing anyone. Kisha said she wasn't dating at the time. Paul mentioned he had a friend named Dexter who wanted to meet someone nice. Kisha wasn't in the habit of going on blind dates but since Paul recommended this guy, she would keep an open mind.

Dexter called Kisha. "Hi, this is Dexter, Paul's friend."

"Hi, how are you doing?" she asked.

"I'm okay, just tired."

"Why are you so tired?" asked Kisha.

"I'm a truck driver, and sometimes when I get home on the weekends, I am very tired, especially if I've been driving long hours."

"I understand. So, what do you do for fun?" she asked.

"I like to go to the movies or chill at home since I'm always travelling. A lot of times all I want is a good home-cooked meal because I eat on the road so much. Can you cook?"

"Yes, I can, and that's understandable, considering the circumstances. What do you like to eat?"

"It really doesn't matter as long as it's home-cooked."

"Okay, then I'll cook for you."

"Good, are you going to bring me the food?"

"Say what? I'm already buying and cooking the food. You mean to tell me you aren't going to come over to eat?"

"I don't feel like driving. You can just bring me a plate."

"Have you lost your damn mind? You don't have a delivery service here. Maybe we can do something when you're not so tired."

"Cool. I'm off this Friday. Do you want to go out for lunch?"

"Okay, Friday sounds like a plan for lunch."

Dexter bragged about how much money he made. He even made it clear that he made more money than she did. He didn't know Kisha came from a prominent family and money was no way to impress her. She was not a gold digger. She had extremely rich relatives that owned bus companies, car dealerships, and funeral homes. Money was never an issue for her, but since he was bragging about his dollar bills, she decided to let him put up or shut up.

They decided to go to a restaurant. She wore a beautiful sundress and sandal heels. Her hair and nails were immaculate. She was dressed to impress. She pulled up to the meeting place and saw a homeless looking character standing out front. She walked right past him and went inside. The homeless guy followed and called her by name. She turned around and saw the guy was wearing a winter sweater and jogging pants in July in Georgia. Who does that? She realized it was Dexter. She was pissed that he hadn't bothered to get dressed to meet her.

Since she was dressed, she decided to at least get the lunch he had promised her. They went to Bone Fish Grill, a nice restaurant. They proceeded to order their food. She conservatively ordered her appetizer and entrée. He ordered a salad.

She says, "Is that all you're going to eat?"

"Yes. I'm not that hungry."

"Okay, but you don't have to be shy around me."

"I'm good."

They began to talk while they waited on their food. He bragged about what he had. Finally, she told him she didn't care about that; she just wanted to get to know him. He, on the other hand, decided to critique her about his impression of her. Kisha was cool, but it seemed like he was trying to do everything he could to irritate her. He didn't realize she was quite classy and was not going to explode on him in public. She began to feel like he was doing that purposely so that she wouldn't want lunch. She was on to his game. She let him talk until they finished eating and the server brought the check. When he paid it, she left, but not before she told him where to go and how to get there with gasoline drawers on. Fifteen minutes later, she passed by him in the drive thru line at McDonald's. She laughed because he knew when he ordered that salad, it wasn't enough.

Resolution

Now, the reason she left was quite simple. The men only met some of her needs with minimal effort. When a woman loves, she will stand beside her man no matter what comes. But when he is the cause of her stress, anxiety, and unhappiness, she will eventually walk away. For some women, it may take longer than others but understand this, she will leave.

Men cannot treat a woman like an object they can pick up and put down at their discretion. She can't be treated like the maid or punching bag. She can't be criticized because of her every flaw. She can't be ignored until sex is wanted. Absentmindedness concerning her feelings like they don't matter or are invalid is intolerable. Her feelings are very real to her.

Ladies, in each story you've read, I'm sure you can relate to the fact that even though the woman loved her man, he was the cause of her leaving. Either his actions, or lack thereof, created an environment not conducive to a lasting relationship.

These stories are true in terms of circumstance and situation. I have witnessed them; some first hand. You must realize that even though the love is real, if she doesn't like him because of his attitude or treatment, she will replace him. He has got to love her and show her. If he is not sure about how to do that, he should ask.

Most women are willing and able to tell a man what they need from him. Just like when they tell her what they want from her sexually, men have to keep an open mind and heart so that they can hear what women need. Below, I have listed some ways that may help keep your relationship building and going.

Suggested Ways to Keep A Relationship Strong

These suggestions are not all that she needs, but they are a good start. This won't guarantee that they will stay but they do ensure a better shot at making it last. There is no money back guarantee, but they do help.

1.   **Pay attention.** Recognize when your mate is not happy with you. Try to put yourself in their shoes and understand how they feel. Make plans to make their days special. Let them know what they mean to you. This is not just in the monetary since, but also quality time.

2.   **Help out.** Children are a major responsibility

whether they are yours or not. Get involved, especially if they *are* yours. If they are a part of your mate's life, then step up if you're going to be a part of theirs.

3.   **Listen.** You are their strength. Your mate should be able to lean on you. Your encouragement and support are essential to a strong relationship.

4.   **Understand what makes them tick.** You should be able to look in their face and know when something isn't right. Know the things that make them smile, cry, laugh, or angry. Your behavior is essential for them to be faithful and willing to stay with you when you are down.

5.   **Keep your word**. People respect those who are honest and keep their word. When your word is valued, then so are you. People will hear your actions over anything you could ever say. This will determine how they respond to you.

6.   **Be dependable**. If your mate needs you, make it your business to be there for them. Sometimes this means physically, mentally, emotionally, or financially. If you have committed to being in the relationship, then you should be totally in it. For ladies, men need to give her emotional stability. For men, ladies need to have their back and they need to know that.

7.   **Pray for your mate.** After watching the movie "War Room," I have learned how important it is to pray.

Complaining and arguing about their shortcomings every time they enter your house won't bring you closer but instead push you farther apart from each other. Your home should be a place of peace. That should be the one place where they know it's a stress free environment. If God isn't the main part of your relationship, then you don't have one.

As a result of writing this book, I realized in each of these relationships, God was not the focus or crucial part. He was completely left out. That's probably why they didn't last. There was no foundation. You can't build anything on quicksand. Any time you try to build any type of relationship without God, it's almost for certain that it won't last. Build your hope on things eternal. Hold to God's unchanging hand.

The End

Contact Me

I love connecting with my readers. Visit me online

Instagram: @The_author_nikki
Facebook @Author Nikki
Or email me at:
Theauthor.nikki@gmail.com

www.ingramcontent.com/pod-product-compliance
Lightning Source LLC
Chambersburg PA
CBHW022044170626
46808CB00003B/1353